SPORTS MYSTERIES

The Secret
of the
Spotted Horse

By Elizabeth Van Steenwyk

Illustrations by Keith Neely

2581

 CHILDRENS PRESS, CHICAGO

Library of Congress Cataloging in Publication Data

Van Steenwyk, Elizabeth.
The secret of the spotted horse.

Summary: When Reddy goes to Montana to visit his
aunt and uncle, he is determined to become a rodeo
champion before the summer is over, but then someone
tries to steal his horse Ruff.
[1. Mystery and detective stories.   2. Horses—
Fiction   3. Rodeos—Fiction] I. Neely, Keith R., ill.
II. Title.
PZ7.V358Se   1983   [Fic]   83-7291
ISBN 0-516-04477-X

The Secret of the Spotted Horse

Chapter 1

Waiting to get out of the airplane at Great Falls, I gave my cowboy boots a shine on the back of my jeans. Then, just before I stepped into the airport, I put on my cowboy hat. I wanted Aunt Biddie and Uncle Wheeler to know I was really serious about becoming a cowboy this summer.

But they weren't doing their part. They didn't look anything at all like ranchers from Box Elder, Montana. They could have been mistaken for almost anyone in Chicago, where I came from. He was wearing a business suit with a tie and a vest and she had on a dress. And a hat. And gloves.

"Been to a weddin'," Aunt Biddie explained when she saw me staring. "But you look like you've been to a costume party."

"I haven't seen angora fur chaps like that since Pioneer Days." Uncle Wheeler laughed.

"I thought this was cowboy country." Now I tried

7

to laugh along with him. "I figured I'd be in the saddle all day. You know, punching cows."

We headed for the baggage carousel downstairs. "I hope our spread won't disappoint you," Uncle Wheeler said. "But we don't have a cow on the place. I'm a wheat farmer."

I nearly lost my balance on the escalator. "Wheat? I thought you'd have horses."

We got my suitcases and started driving north. We drove through miles of open country without a thing on it, not even a tree. Pretty soon it began to seem as if we were the only people left on earth. Finally we turned off the highway and onto a black-top road. Then I saw the mailbox with their name on it, so I knew their house couldn't be far.

I was wrong. "How much farther is it?" I asked after a while.

"We do have a long driveway." Aunt Biddie turned in the front seat to smile at me. "It's five miles to our front porch from the mailbox."

Finally, the house and all the other buildings came in view. It looked almost like a small town.

Uncle Wheeler said, "My ranch manager and his family live in one house. Then those buildings are for tractors and those for combines—"

"We'll show you around," Aunt Biddie said.

Tractors and combines. You'd think they'd have something alive in one of those buildings, I thought.

We pulled up in front of the garage near the boxy white house with red shutters beside every window.

"I want to show you my newest tractor," Uncle Wheeler said. "Come on."

I decided he must not have had any wheel toys when he was a kid. When he opened the door of the big metal building, I was sure of it. I'd never seen so many tractors in my life.

When Uncle Wheeler finally stopped talking long enough to draw a breath, Aunt Biddie interrupted. "Come on, let's go to the barn."

"Barn?" I asked. "I thought you didn't have cows."

"We don't," she replied.

A girl about my size was standing by the barn door when we walked up. Oh, no, they didn't want me to meet her, did they?

"This is our ranch manager's daughter, Idamae George." Aunt Biddie smiled at us. "Idamae, this is our nephew, Redfield Stratton Quigley."

Idamae burst out laughing. "Where did you get a handle like that?"

"Call me Reddy." I tried to look mean.

"You sure are dressed funny," Idamae went on. "Do all Chicagoans wear clothes like that?"

"Idamae," Uncle Wheeler said. "Is your dad around? Did he do what I asked him to do?"

"Yeah, he got it. But he had to get back to the south forty, so he told me to wait for you."

"Let's go inside then." Uncle Wheeler opened the barn door and its earthy cool air greeted us. The only sign of life was a mostly black cat that ambled out of one of the stalls and purred his way around my leg.

"It's your show, Idamae," Aunt Biddie said. "Lead the way."

Idamae turned and headed for the stall at one end of the long, middle corridor. Sure is a big barn, I thought. Sure could have a lot of horses in it, just waiting for me to ride. Then I heard something.

"There he is." Idamae gestured toward the stall in the corner. "He's all yours."

I looked inside. There stood a horse whose white coat was splashed all over with patterns of dark brown hair. He might have been filled out and muscular once, but right now, he was just skinny.

Uncle Wheeler and Aunt Biddie looked into the stall curiously. "Well, now, that's not exactly what I had in mind for Reddy," he began.

"Dad figured you wouldn't want anything too lively for a dude." Idamae eyed my chaps and tried not to giggle. "And Dad said he got a good price."

Uncle Wheeler jingled the change in his pocket. "What kind is he, anyway?"

"Looks like a Paint to me." Idamae said. "But he's a little bigger than your average Paint, so maybe he's got some Quarter in him."

I didn't know what they were talking about; I only knew Idamae said he was all mine.

"Who did your dad say he bought the horse from?" Uncle Wheeler jingled his change some more.

"He didn't say." Idamae leaned against the stall and looked at the horse. "He just said the man was in a hurry to sell and didn't want much. Looks to me like he wanted to sell the horse quick while he was still breathin'."

"Now Idamae," Aunt Biddie said. "I think he'll be just fine for Reddy."

"Yeah, he probably will," she said. "Unless he wants to enter the rodeo or something. Can't you just picture that?" She started giggling.

"Of course I'm going to enter the rodeo." Now I was mad. "And I'm not only going to enter, I'm going to win all around." I just threw that last bit in from something I'd heard on television.

But everything I did was funny to Idamae. When I tore out of the barn, I tripped on my chaps and she just about died laughing.

Chapter 2

I was still steamed at Idamae a few days later and avoided her as much as possible. Now and then I saw her riding her horse and prancing him around some barrels in the yard near her house.

So I just stayed with my own horse and got better acquainted with him. While I was mainly interested in riding, he was mostly interested in eating. So we compromised. He ate and I watched.

"We've really got to decide on your name," I told him, brushing hard. "I can't just go on calling you Horse. Do you like Ruff?"

He just kept right on chewing. "That way we'd be Ruff and Reddy. Get it?"

"You're gonna brush all his hair off."

I jumped about a foot. For a second there, I thought Ruff had started talking. Then I whirled around and saw Idamae.

"Who are you talkin' to anyway?" she asked.

"Nobody here but you and that horse. You're not talkin' to him, are you?"

"Of course not." I brushed harder, which startled Ruff and made him look up.

"Most dudes talk to their horses," Idamae sighed.

There she goes again, I thought. I turned around to really tell her off, then suddenly caught my breath. A streak of sunlight from a crack in the wall was shining on her hair. If she didn't have such a snappy tongue, I realized, she might almost be kind of cute. Her hair was wheat colored and her big brown eyes were fringed with long lashes.

"Your aunt sent me down to fetch you," Idamae said. "Said you two were goin' into Box Elder to buy groceries."

"That's right." I spoke to the horse's shoulder.

"Mind if I tag along?" she asked. "I want to get my entry blank for the rodeo at the feed store. Only got two more days to sign up."

"What rodeo?"

"Fourth of July rodeo." Now she was standing next to me. "This horse sure is funny looking. And look at his hocks. They're all worn."

I wondered where to look for his hocks. Then I saw her looking at his back legs. I leaned down for a better look.

"Hmmmmm." I wondered what to say next.

"What do you think?"

Was she actually asking for my opinion?

"You're probably right." That ought to hold her.

"As soon as Dad comes in from the field tonight, I'm going to ask him more about the man he bought this horse from. I have my suspicions."

What was there to be suspicious about? Maybe she was just trying to impress me.

"Land sakes, you two." It was Aunt Biddie, puffing up the aisle. "I've been callin' and callin'. We've got to get into town before noon."

"Sorry, Aunt Biddie." I put away the brushes I'd been using, gave Ruff an extra pat, and closed the stall door behind me. The mostly black cat followed us to the barn door. We hurried to the station wagon with "Woodward Wheat Farms" printed on its front doors.

"I told your Mama you were goin' with us, Idamae." Aunt Biddie was a good driver and we took right off down the five-mile driveway.

"What rodeo events are you gonna enter?" Idamae said after we'd turned onto the highway.

"Who said I was going to enter?"

"You did, the first day you came." Idamae leaned on the back seat beside me and smiled.

"That was before I knew the condition of my horse. I can't enter the rodeo with a weak horse."

"You can enter the rodeo without any horse at all." Now Idamae's smile could have melted butter. "In fact, you use the rodeo's bucking string for events like bareback and saddle-bronc riding and then you have to use their bull for bull riding."

"Oh, heavens to Betsy, you're not goin' to do that, are you, Reddy?" Aunt Biddie was looking at me in the rearview mirror. "You might get hurt."

"Yeah, you might at that." Idamae kept her face straight. "You probably shouldn't enter at all."

I couldn't tell if she were teasing or being serious. But I sure hated being teased and even worse, not knowing it. "I haven't decided yet," I said.

Aunt Biddie parked in the parking lot of the grocery store. She told us to meet her back at the car in an hour.

Idamae hopped out and turned. "Comin' to sign up?"

"Haven't decided yet." But I walked with her anyway, down the block and into the feed store.

"Mornin', Idamae." A man stood behind the counter, stacking boxes of alfalfa pellets.

"Mornin', Mr. Alston."

"I was wonderin' when you were comin' in to sign

16

up for the rodeo." He handed her an official-looking paper. "The store is the main sponsor of the rodeo again and we aim to make it a lot bigger than last year. So we need all the contestants we can find. Your friend here want to sign up, too?"

"My horse is sick—" I began.

"Don't matter," Mr. Alston interrupted. "You only need him for calf and team ropin' anyway. Why don't you enter somethin' else, like bull ridin'?"

These folks were really serious about getting me killed. "I don't think so," I began.

Now Mr. Alston laughed. "In junior rodeo, they really aren't bulls at all. They're just lil ole steers. You can manage one of them, can't you?"

I looked at Idamae, but she wasn't any help. She just shrugged her shoulders.

Then I thought, if they were just little old steers, like Mr. Alston said, there wasn't anything to be afraid of. Steers are babies, aren't they? Shoot. If I was going to be a cowboy this summer, I had better start pretty soon. And there was no better way to start than by riding baby animals.

I signed up for bull riding. Besides, with Idamae watching and listening, I just had to.

We left the feed store and stood on the porch in the sunshine. Idamae leaned against a couple of feed sacks and nodded to a man sitting on the steps. "What are you gonna name your horse?"

"Thought I'd call him Ruff."

The man turned around and looked us both over. "Got a brand-new horse?"

"Yes." I still couldn't believe Ruff was all mine for the summer. "My uncle gave him to me."

"Nice uncle you got." The man lit a cigarette, then blew smoke through his nose. "Wonder where he got the horse?"

"Her dad bought him—" I began, but suddenly Idamae cut me off.

"Come on, Reddy, your aunt will be waitin' for us." She started down the steps.

"No, she isn't." I looked toward the station wagon. "See, she isn't in the car yet."

Now the man turned to look in the direction of the wagon, with "Woodward Wheat Farms." Then he looked back and smiled. All of a sudden, I didn't want to talk to him any more.

"You're right." I took the steps two at a time, down to Idamae on the sidewalk. "We'd better get back." Then I raced off down the block with Idamae hurrying to keep up. For some reason, I knew I'd done something dumb, really dumb, in blabbing away to that man back on the feed store steps.

18

Chapter 3

I don't know what I expected to happen after talking to that man on the feed store steps. But nothing did, so after a few days, I began to relax.

Besides, Ruff had now declared himself ready to ride and that made me forget everything else. Uncle Wheeler said it was amazing how he recovered his strength so fast and that had to mean he came from good stock. In fact, his good bloodline advertised itself in everything he did. Uncle Wheeler still couldn't understand why he'd gotten him so cheap.

"Come on, Ruff," I said, leading him from the barn. Learning how to put on his bridle and saddle hadn't been easy, but everybody on the ranch was more than willing to help me. Except Idamae. She just stood around and watched while Ruff and I took lessons: Ruff on patience, me on saddling.

Today, Uncle Wheeler planned to start teaching me calf roping. Of course we didn't have a calf, so I was going to practice roping the fence post instead.

"The horse is as important as you are in this event," Uncle Wheeler said. "Cowboys want horses that are intelligent and agile enough to stop on a dime. Why don't you let me ride him a minute and test him out? Your old uncle used to be one of the best ropers in the state of Montana."

I handed over the reins. Then Uncle Wheeler heaved himself up on Ruff. Now a few of the hands and Aunt Biddie had joined Idamae to watch him demonstrate. But it didn't bother Uncle Wheeler.

"Whoa, Ruff, steady," he said, as my horse pawed the ground. "Now I'm goin' to try to lasso that post over there." He pointed towards the fence near the barn. He tied one end of the rope to his saddle horn and then carried the rest of it, looped, in his free hand.

Now he tapped Ruff's stomach with his heels and said "Giddayap" and Ruff began to move. Really move. Yikes.

Uncle Wheeler headed him for the fence post and when he got just the right distance from it, he swung the rope around in the air and zap, over it went and tied up the post, neat as you please.

But he wasn't through yet. Uncle Wheeler hopped down from Ruff and made him hold the rope taut somehow. Then ran to the post and tied it again with a smaller rope. Then Uncle Wheeler threw his hands straight up in the air and called, "Time."

Everybody started clapping. Uncle Wheeler rode Ruff over to us, grinning with pleasure. He got down and mopped his face with a red handkerchief before he said, "Still a little spark left in the old man. Now you do it, Reddy."

Just like that. You do it, Reddy. Oh, boy. I climbed up on Ruff who suddenly seemed to have grown a mile taller. Then Uncle Wheeler showed me how to tie one end of the rope to the saddle horn and hold the rest of it looped in my free hand. Free hand. I needed at least two hands to hold on to the reins. What free hand? But I found one.

"This here's the piggin' string." Uncle Wheeler held a short, softer-looking rope out to me. "This is what you'll tie the calf's feet together with, or in our case, the post."

"Where do I carry that?"

"In your mouth," Uncle Wheeler said and jammed the rope between my teeth.

"Now, go." Uncle Wheeler slapped Ruff's rump and my horse obliged, heading straight for the fence.

One thing soon became clear to me. I didn't know when to stop, or how to, for that matter. But the closer that fence got, the more it seemed like I'd better figure that part out. And soon.

Then I put it all together in a split second. Ruff thought he was that fancy white horse with wings and we were going to fly right over the fence. The next thing I knew I really was flying, but I was doing a solo. It was just me sailing over the fence.

"Reddy, are you all right?" Uncle Wheeler and Aunt Biddie came puffing up to the fence. I could see Idamae out of the corner of my eye.

"I'm just fine." But as soon as I climbed to the top of the fence, Ruff and I had an eyeball-to-eyeball discussion. "That's the last time you dump this dude, hear?"

"Let's try it again," Uncle Wheeler said. And he got me back on Ruff and made me try roping that fence post at least ten more times until he was satisfied. By now most of my audience had left.

Then a miracle happened. The last time I tried it, my rope actually tied up the fence post.

"Atta boy," Uncle Wheeler yelled. "Now run down the line and tie that doggie."

I ran hand over hand along the taut rope, as he showed me. I pretended I was roping a mean old calf. Then I threw my hands in the air and yelled "Time" the same way Uncle Wheeler did.

"That's great," he yelled, coming over and hugging me so hard he knocked the wind out of me. "And I got to admire your spunk, too, Reddy. You came right back and kept tryin'."

I led Ruff back to the stall. I hurt all over from riding and roping. But it was fun.

I practiced hard every day after that, with Idamae looking on from a distance. If she knew how to rope a calf or a fence post, she didn't offer any advice. She just watched and listened to Uncle Wheeler. He patiently took me through the event again and again and again. Idamae sure was cute though.

One morning Uncle Wheeler announced that he had to go to Missoula to see about a new tractor.

"Not another one, Wheeler," Aunt Biddie said.

"Yep. Be back in a day or two," was all he would say. Half an hour later, he disappeared down the five-mile driveway in his pickup truck.

Thunder woke me the next night. A crack of lightning zigzagged across the sky. Aunt Biddie's fancy curtains danced at the open window. I should close it before they get wet, I thought.

But before I got the window closed, something moved across the sill on the outside. I froze. What was it? Suddenly a dark body leaped through the flapping curtains and onto my bed.

"You got a lot of nerve," I whispered to the mostly black cat, now washing himself and purring at the same time. "Scare me like that again and I won't save you any more liver."

I went back to the window and stuck my head out. I got a blast of rain in my face. But just before I pulled back inside, I saw the branch of the cottonwood tree that touched the side of the house right beside my bedroom window. That cat ought to join the circus and do a high-wire act, I thought.

Then it hit me that I'd seen something else in that glance out the window. Holy cats. I began to get really scared now. I shivered as if I were in a high wind. Finally, I dared a second glance outside.

Someone was walking carefully and quietly towards the buildings where Uncle Wheeler kept his machinery. A big raincoat covered him like a blanket—or was that a disguise? Who could it be?

Then I thought of the man on the feed store steps. Didn't he wear a hat like that? And didn't he seem interested in Idamae and me? Maybe he was out to steal some of Uncle Wheeler's expensive machinery. Wouldn't everybody be impressed if I sounded the alarm? Everybody, especially Idamae?

Chapter 4

I raced down the hall to Aunt Biddie's room and barely knocked before charging inside. "Aunt Biddie," I whispered. "Someone's prowling around outside."

She sat up in bed, hair curlers framing her face like a weird space helmet. "Land sakes," she said. "I'd better call Sam."

While she dialed Idamae's dad, I watched out the window for more suspicious activity. The thunderclouds were so thick now that they covered the moon and the stars. But whenever there was a flash of lightning, I caught a peek of strange goings-on through the leafy branches of the cottonwood trees.

Then it occurred to me. How do you steal a tractor? Do you just drive it out of the machinery shed or what? That must be what all the activity was about.

"Sam said he'd be right over." Aunt Biddie pulled

her furry robe close to her. "Let's go down to the kitchen and wait."

We hurried downstairs in the dark, after I cautioned Aunt Biddie that we shouldn't use lights and alert the thief. We wanted to catch him red-handed.

Sam must have had the same idea about not alerting anyone, because in a minute or less, he was at the back door in the dark, and knocking quietly. Aunt Biddie unlocked the door and let him in.

He looked sleepy and his black poncho was sleek with rain. "Now where did you see the burglar?" he asked me, balancing a shotgun over his arm.

"Heading for the biggest machinery shed," I whispered. "There's something really strange moving around out there. Do you suppose they've brought a gang to push the tractor down—"

"Heavens to Betsy," Aunt Biddie interrrupted. "Maybe we ought to call the sheriff."

"Let me have a look around first," Sam said. "But call the bunkhouse, Mrs. Woodward, and roust a couple of the boys, just in case I need any help. If we're not back in five minutes, call the sheriff."

Aunt Biddie went off to call the bunkhouse. I watched as Sam slipped out into the rain, trying to hide in the shadows of bushes and trees around the house and barn. Then I lost him.

"Where did he go?" I whispered to the curtain. Suddenly the yard lights flooded the driveway and I saw Sam running into the metal building where Uncle Wheeler kept his biggest combine. A couple of hands dashed through the rain from another direction and disappeared inside, too. Lightning flashed and thunder rolled as I shivered with cold and excitement. I should have gone along for the capture.

Now the building door opened wide and I strained to see the thief. There was Sam first, then the boys from the bunkhouse and then—oh, no. It was Uncle Wheeler.

They came back to the kitchen and Sam stuck his head inside the door. Dripping with rain and sarcasm, he told me, "Here's your thief, young man. Next time, when you want excitement, watch the late show."

Uncle Wheeler took off his dripping raincoat, and hung his soaked hat on a peg before he started in on his boots.

"I really appreciate your lookin' out for things," Uncle Wheeler said, as I hoped the floor would cave in and make me disappear. "But I just don't appreciate havin' a shotgun pointed at my middle."

"I'm sorry, Uncle Wheeler. I thought—"

"That's all right, young man. I was bein' kind of

skulky at that. You see, I was so anxious to get back and show you what I bought, that I drove straight through. I shoulda called Biddie, but I wanted to surprise her, too."

"Another tractor isn't the biggest surprise around here," said Aunt Biddie.

"Didn't buy a tractor." Uncle Wheeler grinned so hard that his eyes closed. "Bought a calf for the boy to rope and stashed him in among the tractors, so it'd be a real surprise."

"A calf?" I yelled. "A real live calf? Can I go see him now?"

Uncle Wheeler laughed. "Best wait till mornin' so you won't get nabbed for a tractor snatcher." That hurt, but I still went to sleep happy.

The morning air was pure after the storm and I headed for the metal building as soon as breakfast was over. But Idamae had beat me there.

"I had to see what all the excitement was about last night," she said. She didn't laugh exactly, but her eyes were glittering.

The calf was tied to a tractor and eating something from a pail. Probably dynamite so he could buck and rear, judging from the look in his eyes.

"Better to be safe than sorry," I told Idamae.

"You're probably right. Need some help with him?"

"Do you really want to help me or do you just want to hang around for laughs?" I wanted to be friends with her, but we just had to get a few things settled first.

She turned on me, daggers in her voice. "If you're too proud to take help from a girl, just let me know. I got practicin' of my own to do for the rodeo."

"That's not what I meant and you know it." I stared at the calf who stared back. "I'm just tired of being laughed at."

"Then stop doin' such funny things." She started giggling again.

"See, there you go—"

"I'm sorry, I promise, no more laughin'." She held her hand in the air in a kind of Brownie salute. "No kiddin', I know how to do most of the rodeo events. I'm pretty good. I won barrel racin' last time and—"

Now it was my turn to laugh. "Barrel racing? What do you do, put on barrels and run as fast as you can? Or does your horse wear the barrels?"

"Very funny." She turned up her nose. "I just thought that since we were right here on the same ranch, we could practice together. I plan to enter calf ropin' too so I can go for the All Around for girls."

"So now you want to borrow my calf, is that it?"

That didn't sound very nice, but I didn't know how to take it back.

"No, that's not it." Now she patted my calf as he ate. "There's one event that I thought we could do together, in fact you have to have a partner. I figured that way you could really be a contender—"

"Are you trying to tell me I won't be able to win without your help?"

"You really are dumb," she said. "I'm tryin' to keep you from makin' a fool of yourself in the Fourth of July rodeo and this is the thanks I get."

Now we were nose to nose, both of us mad as yellow jackets. "I'll show you who's going to make a fool out of himself in the rodeo." I turned on my heel and ran over to the barn where I saddled up Ruff in record time. I was on his back and out of the barn just in time to see a car pull up into the yard. Ida-mae watched as a man and a woman got out and approached Ruff and me.

"Good morning, young man." The lady was all smeary lipstick and sunglasses. "I wonder if you can help me." She began to stroke Ruff's nose.

"I'll try."

Now the man began to look at Ruff carefully. "What kind of horse you got here, Sonny?" He ran his hands over Ruff's sides and down his legs.

"You'll have to ask my uncle about his breed." I looked at Idamae and she shrugged her shoulders before she quietly walked up behind them. "Are you folks looking for someone special?" I asked.

"We seem to be lost." The lady turned around and noticed Idamae for the first time. "My brother works at the Bar El Ranch, herding cattle—"

"This is the Woodward Wheat Farms." Idamae was as sweet as sugar. "But if you'll wait a minute, we can phone over to the Bar El and see if your brother is there or if he's gone on the cattle drive."

"Oh, no, we want to surprise him." The lady smiled her smeary smile. "Come on, Harry." They headed for their car before Idamae stopped them.

"Don't you want to know how to get there?"

"Oh, yes, of course." They listened politely while Idamae gave them directions.

"They sure came a long way off the highway to ask about the Bar El." I tried to hold Ruff still.

Idamae had the weirdest look on her face before she spoke. "The Bar El is a wheat farm, like this one. They haven't run cattle over there for years. Isn't that funny?"

I nodded, full of surprise. Idamae had run right into something else that was funny—only this time, she wasn't laughing.

Chapter 5

The Fourth of July seemed to arrive two weeks early. I wasn't ready to go to the rodeo, much less participate in it. At least the calf and I knew who was the boss. He was. I needed more practice, maybe ten years' worth. But it was too late to back out now. Idamae would never get over laughing at that. Besides, Mr. Alston at the feed store let me sign up late for the calf roping event, so I had to show up. And then there was my aunt and uncle.

"You're not eatin'." Aunt Biddie stared in amazement at my still-full breakfast plate.

"Guess I'm too excited."

"Once you get out there in the arena today, all your nerves will disappear," Uncle Wheeler said, helping himself to another slab of fried ham.

"We're real proud of you, Reddy," Aunt Biddie beamed. "To come out here from Chicago and jump right into rodeoin' right off. That takes real spunk."

I was too weak to do anything more than smile. But come to think of it, maybe I ought to talk, make some kind of noise so nobody could hear my knees knocking together.

"Uncle Wheeler, did you ever ask Sam who sold him Ruff?"

Uncle Wheeler put sugar in his coffee and stirred it slowly while he answered. "Yes. He said he met this fella in the feed store who was fixin' to advertise on that bulletin board Mr. Alston's got set up inside. They got to talkin' about his horse for sale. When Sam looked at Ruff, he snapped him up for you because the horse was such a bargain. Why?"

"Just curious." I watched Uncle Wheeler test his coffee before I went on. "Why would someone get rid of a good horse like Ruff with just a notice in the feed store? You said Ruff had good bloodlines and he sure attracts his share of attention."

"How do you mean, attention?" Uncle Wheeler considered the plate of fresh cinnamon rolls Aunt Biddie had just placed in the middle of the table.

"A man and woman came by a week or so ago looking for her brother, but when they saw Ruff, they seemed more interested in him than anything else."

"Maybe they recognized him as a Paint with outstanding markings."

"You mean he really might be a valuable horse, worth a lot of money?" Something was clicking away in my brain. "Maybe that fella back in the feed store might have made a mistake in selling him to Sam."

Uncle Wheeler put his coffee cup down and stared at me. "Maybe he made the mistake before he sold him to Sam," he said slowly. "Maybe his mistake was in actin' like the horse was his to sell in the first place."

You could have driven a truck into my mouth, the way it dropped open. Before I had time to think, Aunt Biddie stood up and announced, "Time to go, you two."

"Let's put Ruff in his trailer." Uncle Wheeler rolled a toothpick around in his mouth as he spoke, still thinking over what we'd just said, I could tell.

I followed him out to Ruff's stall and got all the gear together. Then Uncle Wheeler and I put him in the trailer already hitched to the station wagon. A few minutes later Aunt Biddie joined us with two overflowing picnic baskets that she stowed beside me on the back seat. Finally we took off down the driveway to the fairgrounds and my doom.

The action had already started in the big arena when we got there. In spite of my fear, I began to get excited. Maybe, I thought. Maybe everything will turn out okay when I draw the slowest calf and the sleepiest steer in Montana for my events.

We unloaded Ruff in a stall under the grandstand and I began to brush him down. Dust stirred up by all the contestants and animals got in my eyes and nose and I sneezed several times.

"Bless you." It was Idamae, all dressed up in new jeans and a western hat. "Ready, Reddy?"

"Sure." I tried to play it cool like Ruff.

"Barrel racin's next," she said. "Wish me luck." She took off on her horse toward the arena entrance.

I followed her and stood beside the fence as Idamae confidently took her horse into the arena. She rode him around three barrels that were the points of an imaginary triangle. In no time, she was back, all smiles as people around us congratulated her.

"Calf ropin's the next event," she called to me. "Now I'll wish you luck."

I sure needed it. Ruff and I rode into the ring as if we knew what we were doing. That was the best part. When the calf was released at the other end of the arena, I touched Ruff's flanks with my boots and we started off. I actually had my rope whirling in the air, ready to lasso the calf. But we rode right by him.

"Doggone it, Ruff." I turned him around, sweating under my shirt. "You know better." We headed for the calf again, who eyed us with suspicion. According to the rules, I got two chances to rope him, but first I had to get close enough. Suddenly, the calf charged us. Ruff turned tail and ran the full length of the arena with that calf right at our heels.

I could hear the audience all the way out to Ruff's stall. Now it wasn't only Idamae but half the state of Montana laughing at me.

"You really goofed," I told Ruff as I unsaddled him. But I knew who had made the biggest mistake. Me, for thinking I could do any of this cowboy stuff.

Bull riding was the next event. At least, I'd have a chance here, with just a little baby steer to worry about. When my name was called, I walked over and climbed up on the top of the chute where the animals are kept and looked down. But when I looked down, that wasn't a baby animal staring up at me.

"Somebody made a mistake," I yelled to the handler. "I'm supposed to be riding a steer."

"That ain't no giraffe, Sonny." The handler looked at me as if I didn't have good sense. He showed me how to grab the handhold that was tied to a rope that went around the steer's middle.

"You can only use one hand, Sonny," the handler said. "And hang on for six seconds, or it's no contest."

Then he released the gate and the steer shot out into the arena with me holding on with as much ability as one of Mr. Alston's feed sacks.

"It's wrong-way Reddy, back again," the announcer shouted into the loudspeaker as we bucked our way around the ring.

The handler was right. It wasn't any contest. I landed on my backside in no time at all. There is a bright side to bull riding though. It doesn't last long. And my steer didn't hold a grudge. Once he got rid of me he ambled back to the chute, while I limped my way through the contestant's entrance. Idamae was waiting there by the door.

"Got to hand it to you," she said. "You sure got spunk."

If one more person told me I had spunk today, I was going to throw up.

"You don't look too happy." Idamae gave me a long look from under her new hat.

"I'm through." I kicked at a rock as we headed back to Ruff's stall.

"You sure give up easy."

"What do you expect me to do?"

"Try harder."

"So you and the rest of Montana can laugh?" I kicked at another rock.

"I take it back. You don't have any spunk at all. You're just a big crybaby. And just like that, you're quittin'."

"Unless you got a better idea."

"You and me can be a team. We'll be team ropers and take first prize, I know we will."

"The rodeo's over."

"A bigger one's comin' in a couple of weeks. Frontier Days is the best in the state."

I studied her face while I made up my mind, knowing I wanted to be a cowboy more than anything else in the world. I guessed it was worth being laughed at a few more times. But could I do it? Maybe not, but I'd never know until I tried, would I?

"You've got a deal," I said. "How much time do we have to turn me into a first-rate roper?"

"Time enough." Suddenly she glanced past my shoulder. "Hey," she said. "Where's that guy takin' Ruff?"

"What guy?" I whirled around. It was the guy we'd talked to on the feed store steps, leading Ruff out of the stall. When he saw me, he dropped the reins and began to run as I started chasing him.

"Stop him," I yelled at anyone who would listen. "He tried to steal my horse!"

Chapter 6

A few days later, I was still thinking about the nerve of that guy trying to steal Ruff at the rodeo. Somehow he'd managed to disappear in the crowd and noboby knew who he was or where to look for him. He was really a mystery man.

Idamae had just put me through a morning's workout designed to make a team roper out of me or kill me in the attempt. At the moment, I was too tired to do anything else but sit in the sunshine. I let my mind wander back to the mystery man. He really must be desperate to get Ruff back. Where would he strike next? In spite of the warm sunshine, goosebumps crept along my spine.

Uncle Wheeler was right, though. Ruff hadn't been that man's to sell in the first place, or he wouldn't have been sneaking around at the rodeo, trying to steal him back. I had two questions in my mind. Who owned Ruff? And why was he stolen? If I knew, I could call the owner up and tell him his horse was safe with me. Of course, that meant I'd have to spend the rest of the summer without Ruff.

"Come on, Reddy." Idamae galloped up on her chestnut gelding. "Rest time is over. Let's get back to work on our team ropin'."

No point in arguing with Idamae when she's bossy, so I swung up on Ruff and followed along the fence line.

Ed, who works for Uncle Wheeler, walked up to us now carrying a can of paint.

"You two gonna enter the team ropin' contest?" Ed opened the can of paint and studied it, waiting for it to change color, I guess.

"Yep," Idamae said. "What are you gonna paint?"

"The fence, here," Ed said. "Mr. Woodward likes it brand, spankin' white." He dipped his brush into the paint and took a swipe at the top railing. "You kids look out now that you don't come along here till the paint's dry."

"Right." I started to move Ruff away from the fence.

"And pay attention to Idamae, Reddy." When he pointed at me with his brush, some paint dripped on the ground. "She's a good little roper and you're learnin' fast. You two will be hard to beat at the rodeo next week."

That did it. With Ed's words buzzing in her head, Idamae ran me and the calf ragged for the next hour. Try to picture what we were doing. Right now, in practice, we're chasing our little calf in the meadow. But in the rodeo a full-size steer is released into the arena. Then a second later, two rope-swinging cowboys come bursting out of the barriers in hot pursuit. That's us, Idamae and me. All we have to do is rope this wild-eyed steer with horns.

Horns. That's my end. I'm the header because Idamae says it's easier to rope the horns than his hind feet, which is why she's the heeler. Of course, our little calf doesn't have any horns, I just have to imagine they're there and lasso his neck while I'm in the saddle. Nothing to it.

We practice this for an hour and once in a while I really do it, really do lasso the calf and pull him to a stop so Idamae can swing in under his hind legs with her rope. It doesn't hurt the calf any, but it isn't his idea of what to do on a Thursday afternoon either. When we release him, he takes off like he's been shot out of a cannon.

"Not bad." Idamae wiped her face with a bandana. "And Ruff sure has learned his job in a hurry, holdin' the rope nice and taut like that while I do my part."

We headed for the barn and brushed our horses down, then Idamae put her gelding in the stall next to Ruff's. After we threw hay into their stalls, we went back outside.

My mind drifted back to the mystery of Ruff's ownership. "Remember that man and woman who came by, looking for her brother?" I asked.

"Yeah. What made you think of them?"

"They acted funny. It seemed to me they weren't really looking for her brother."

"Yeah, me too."

"They seemed more interested in Ruff than anything else."

"Right."

"What if somebody stole their horse?" I started to lean against the fence, then thought better of it. "What if they were looking for their stolen horse when they came by here?"

"Why didn't they say so?" Idamae asked. "And why didn't they recognize Ruff if he had been stolen from them?"

"Maybe they're trying to catch the thief themselves and maybe they didn't know Ruff because—he looked different." I knew those were crazy answers to her questions but it was the best I could do. Remember, I'm a dude.

"Well, if they're lookin for a horse, stolen or otherwise, they'll be at the rodeo." Idamae fanned herself with her hat.

"Why?"

"Everybody who is anybody in the horse business will be there. That's what my dad says anyway."

Now Idamae looked down the road to her own house and groaned. Her mother was standing on the porch, waving at her. "I have to go. Mom's givin' me the high sign about doin' chores."

That night, before I went to bed, I opened the window wide so the mostly black cat could come in when he got sleepy. He'd been staying out later and later these nights as the weather warmed up, but was always at the foot of the bed when I woke up in the morning. Sometimes I heard him come in and sometimes I didn't.

I figured it was the cat coming in when I woke up around two, but he wasn't there. Then I turned over to see if he was standing on the windowsill, but it was empty, so I tried to figure out what had jangled my brain to wake me up. These days I was so tired from Idamae's lessons that I usually slept like a load of bricks had fallen on me.

Then I began to think about the mystery man. Had he come back for another try at stealing my horse? Listen, was that a whinny coming from the barn?

I got up and listened, tensing up as another noise rustled the night air. There was nothing to see in the barnyard. But maybe the thief was already inside, putting on Ruff's halter and getting ready to lead him away. Best to tell Uncle Wheeler, I thought.

I tiptoed down the hall to his bedroom and stood with my hand on the door knob, but I didn't knock. What if I got everybody up again and this time captured somebody real dangerous like Aunt Biddie? I'd never live it down, not this time.

I let my breath out in a deep sigh and tiptoed downstairs to the kitchen. This would have to be a one-man job, and I'd just been elected. Aunt Biddie's small flashlight was in the drawer by the sink and I took it, as much for protection as for light.

When I got to the barn door, I waited and listened. There was no sound, no light, nothing but quiet now. The door cooperated without so much as a squeak. I stepped inside and let my eyes grow accustomed to the darkness.

Now I waited for something to happen. Let someone else make the first move. I'm no hero. I'm not even a first-class coward.

Ruff was restless and pawed around in his stall and now Idamae's horse was doing it, too. If they could only tell me what it was. But maybe they were. Maybe they were warning me—

What was that? There, over in the vacant stall on the other side of Ruff. A sound, a funny, little—I tiptoed over, ready to strike—

"Meow." Oh, no. It was the mostly black cat, his eyes glowing in the corner of the dark, vacant stall.

"What's the matter?" I went over to pet him and my hand came away sticky. What was it? Blood, maybe. Maybe he'd been hurt. I fumbled for the flashlight and shone it over him, but he wasn't mostly black anymore. He had big patches of white paint on his paws and his ears where he'd probably tried to wash it off. Now it must hurt him. Poor guy.

"Come on, let's clean you up, fast." I knew there was paint thinner in the equipment shed. It would probably sting a little, but the paint would kill him for sure if he tried to lick any more of it off.

I stopped by Ruff's stall and shone the flashlight on him just long enough to make sure he was all right, when an idea staggered me so much that my knees turned weak.

Chapter 7

I hurried to the equipment shed, using my flashlight as little as possible, and cleaned off the mostly
black cat with paint thinner. Then I washed him with
soap and water before turning him loose. Was he
ever happy to get away from me.

But I couldn't think about that now. My idea was
driving me crazy. I hurried back to Ruff's stall with
soap and water and started to work by flashlight, but
that was a waste of time. When I turned on the
overhead light in the stall, for a second Ruff and I
blinked at one another in the sudden brightness.

I didn't know where to begin on Ruff, so I started
on the back end and examined his markings up
close. Then I attacked the big brown splotches of
color on his rump with soap and water and they
began to disappear with just a little scrubbing.

When I washed down his legs, another big splotch
came away. Before I finished about an hour later, I'd

gone all over him, checking for any more paint or unusual markings. I found one more. Just where his right front leg joins his body, I found a number, a kind of tattoo, branded there. It was so small that you had to be looking real hard to find it.

"Hey, Ruff, you've got your own I.D." I patted him now as I threw a blanket over his back. "I've always known you were someone special." When I went to bed, I was really high on myself.

The next morning I dreamed I was riding a bull, rocking and rolling and tossing and turning, but I was hanging on and winning! Me, the dude from the city, was actually winning. I had ridden longer than the required six seconds, my time was sixty minutes, the all-time national championship for bull riding. The announcer was shouting over the microphone and the audience was cheering, calling my name over and over and over—

"Reddy—Reddy—wake up. You gonna sleep all day?"

I opened my eyes and stared up into Aunt Biddie's face.

"You were sleepin' so hard I thought I'd have to roll you out on the floor to wake you up. When you didn't come down for breakfast, I began to worry that you might be sick."

I threw back the covers, revealing my dirty, smelly pajamas.

"I'm okay, Aunt Biddie, it's just that—"

She wrinkled up her nose. "What smells?"

"It's only paint thinner. That's what I started—"

"Paint thinner?" She looked puzzled.

Suddenly I knew I had to catch Uncle Wheeler before he went to the fields. "Yeah, I had to wash the mostly black cat. Where's Uncle Wheeler? I got something important to tell him."

Now Aunt Biddie looked at me as if I'd grown warts. "What's so important about washing the cat in paint thinner that you have to tell Uncle Wheeler in such a hurry? I admit it's different—"

I couldn't stop to explain, but dashed downstairs to the kitchen. Uncle Wheeler was just walking out the back door. "Uncle Wheeler," I yelled.

He turned around and pushed his western hat back on his head. "Mornin', Reddy. We gave up on you and had our breakfast already. What's up?"

"I have to talk to you," I began.

Aunt Biddie hurried into the room. "Wait a minute, Reddy. If you're goin' to tell Wheeler about the cat and the paint thinner, I got to hear it too."

We sat down at the table, but I didn't eat right away. I was too busy telling about finding the cat with the painted legs and figuring out that maybe Ruff might be a Paint in more ways than one. "And sure enough, he was," I finished. "When I scrubbed him with soap and water, some of his spots came off, too."

"The old vegetable dye trick," Uncle Wheeler said, rolling a toothpick around in his mouth. "That's a trick so old I never would have suspected anyone of doin' it in this day and age. Good thing he wasn't left out in the rain." He began to chuckle.

"But why would that man paint Ruff to disguise him if he was going to sell him so cheap?"

"Maybe the thief didn't have a chance to sell him to the people he planned to." Uncle Wheeler chomped away on his toothpick. "Or maybe he didn't know what a valuable horse he had."

I stared at the sausage and scrambled eggs Aunt Biddie had put on my plate. "Then why steal him?"

Uncle Wheeler leaned back on two legs of his chair. "You sure do ask good questions, Reddy," he said. "But I can't answer that one, so maybe we ought to let the sheriff try." He brought his chair back to its right position. "I'll go see him right now."

"Why don't you just call him?" Aunt Biddie asked.

Uncle Wheeler's chuckle grew louder, like thunder in his throat. "I got to see his face when I start tellin' about the cat and the paint thinner." He stood up and headed for the door. "Besides, I got to go to town anyway to see about a part for the combine."

"Can I go with you, Uncle Wheeler?"

"Sure, Reddy. Meet you outside in fifteen minutes." He was still laughing when he slammed the back door behind him.

Later that afternoon, Idamae was waiting down by the barn when Uncle Wheeler and I got back.

"Where were you?" she asked. "I thought we were gonna practice this mornin'."

"I'm sorry I'm late, but wait till I tell you whom I've been talking to." I hurried into my story about calling on the sheriff and describing the mystery man for him and laid it on thick to impress Idamae.

"Why didn't you ask me to go with you?" Idamae looked ready to pop. "After all, I was the first one to be suspicious of the mystery man."

By now we were in the barn, walking toward Ruff's stall. "Uncle Wheeler had to hurry, Idamae, so I couldn't call you. But I'll get Ruff now and we can start right in on our practice."

Idamae didn't act as if she'd heard me. "Look at your horse," she whispered. "He looks so different. What happened—what did you do?"

"I washed him, that's all." I drew a line in the dirt with the toe of my boot, trying to act really cool.

"But, how did you know your horse was disguised?" Idamae looked impressed.

I took off my western hat and examined the crease carefully. "We dudes know more about horses than we're given credit for."

She looked at me for a second or two, almost taken in by my act before she began to laugh and throw hay in my face. "Oh, yeah? I've taught you everything you know about horses and don't you forget it."

Then I confessed how the mostly black cat helped me become the great detective, before we started our workout. As we practiced, I tried not to think that today might be one of the last times I'd get to ride Ruff.

A couple of days later at supper time, Aunt Biddie told me to call the sheriff. "He's got some news for you," she said.

I dialed the number and soon the sheriff's voice boomed into the receiver. "Howdy, young man." It sounded as if he were broadcasting from the next room. "Thanks to you, we caught ourselves a gen-u-wine horse thief."

"Just like in the movies." I tried to force some enthusiasm.

"That's right. We found the guy and he confessed right away. Nothin' to it, Reddy."

"What did he say?"

"He said he stole the horse from the man and woman he used to work for. Then he gave the horse a paint job to disguise his looks before he sold him to Sam."

"Why did he try to steal Ruff back?"

"He didn't learn how valuable a horse he was until he saw the ad in *Western Horse* magazine, about Painted Horse Farms. That's out in Idaho. They had your horse's picture in the ad, so that's when he decided to steal him back and make some real money."

"Do you want us to call that farm?" Reddy began.

"You let me handle it," the sheriff said. "And wait for proof of ownership before you hand over that horse to anybody. He's worth his weight in gold."

I hung up, trying to be happy that Ruff's real owners had been found. But it was hard. Saying good-bye to Ruff wouldn't be easy. And there was something that kept nagging away at me the rest of the evening. What was it that I had forgotten that was so important to remember?

Chapter 8

The morning of Frontier Days rodeo arrived too soon. Ever since the mystery man had been captured, I waited for the owners of Ruff to contact us. I wanted to make the most of my remaining time with him. Naturally, I wasn't ready to give him up today or any day. But still the owners hadn't called and Uncle Wheeler said they might be on a trip or something. Now it looked as if my chances to ride Ruff in the rodeo this afternoon were good. Even if they came today, they'd let me ride before they took him home, wouldn't they?

"Sure they will," Idamae said, as we were packing our gear in the barn. "It would give them a great chance to show off their horse before thousands of people."

"Thousands?" I'd never thought of that before. Thousands were going to watch me try to rope a steer? Oh, boy.

"Well, maybe close to a thousand." Idamae glanced over and saw me frozen in place. "Don't sweat it, Reddy. Come on, help me get the horses in the trailer."

I swallowed hard and followed her out, leading Ruff. I had enough pressure on me and now all those people to think about, too. People were going to expect so much from me, being Uncle Wheeler's nephew and all. Maybe I should have worn a disguise, maybe a mask over my face, so no one would know me. We definitely shouldn't be wearing these denim shirts with "Woodward Wheat Farms" embroidered on the back of them. That had been Aunt Biddie's gift to us. Maybe the last gift of my short, uneventful life, I thought, as we headed down the five-mile driveway to the rodeo and the steer who had my name embroidered on his horns.

"Isn't this fun?" Idamae said a little later, as we put Ruff and her gelding in our assigned stalls.

"Yeah, fun." There really was a lot to look at, but it didn't impress me much. All those colored streamers on poles outlining the arena, all the kids and their parents wandering around visiting and cracking jokes should have been exciting, but I couldn't raise my spirits. Giving up Ruff was the pits.

Uncle Wheeler leaned in over the dutch door of

the stall and held out a couple of hot dogs painted with mustard. "Got to keep up your strength," he said. Idamae gobbled hers up and then mine too, when I said I wasn't hungry.

"You want to visit around?" Idamae wiped mustard from her chin.

"No, think I'll stay with Ruff."

"Listen for the band," she said. "When they play the national anthem, get ready, because team ropin's the first event." She disappeared into the crowd and I leaned against the dutch door, watching. Ruff nudged me a couple of times and snuffled around my ears. I wondered if he knew he was going home soon and that was his way of saying good-bye.

Suddenly Ruff's owners appeared by the corner of the grandstand. It was almost as if they'd stepped out of a curtain on stage. They were just there, walking straight towards me out of the crowd.

"Hey," I yelled. But they couldn't hear me because of all the noise. Now they were turning in another direction, and I ran after them. Best to let them know their horse is safe with me.

"Remember me?" They stopped to stare at me now. "You came by Woodward Wheat Farms—" I turned around so they could see my embroidered back, then faced them again.

They looked at me and then at one another, puzzled, I guess. "I knew what you wanted when you came driving up that day," I lied.

"Look, Harry." The woman finally found her voice as she stared over my head at Ruff.

"I figured out how Ruff had been disguised and why." I bragged it up some more.

"Pretty smart kid," Harry said.

"Yeah, I knew the horse was stolen," I went on. "And when you didn't come back, I told the sheriff—"

"Sheriff?" The woman looked surprised.

"Look, Sonny," Harry said. "Why don't we go back to our trailer and get this settled?"

"Okay," I nodded my head. "But if you'll call the sheriff, he can set you straight in no time. Guess you've been out of town."

"Yeah," Harry replied. "We'll call him as soon as we get to the trailer."

"I suppose you've got proof of ownership there." I followed him.

"Oh, yes," the woman said behind me.

As I walked, that funny nagging feeling started in again. I knew there was something I should remember, but right now I was too excited to concentrate.

The minute I stepped into the trailer with number

321 attached to the door, I remembered. "Why
didn't you check Ruff's number that day at the
ranch?"

"Number?" the woman asked.

"Yeah, his tattoo number, under—" But if they
were his owners, why didn't they know about his
tattoo? Why was I telling them something they
should know? Oh, boy. I'd done it again. Opened my
mouth and let it flap once too often.

Slowly, I edged my way to the door. "Got to run."

"He knows, Harry," the woman said.

"Ruff isn't your horse either," I said, wishing my
mouth would stop. "You stole him, too, and then the
mystery man stole him from you."

"But we know the horse is a champion sire and
worth thousands, when we get him to Canada."
Harry took a step towards me. "And nobody's gonna
stand in our way between here and the border."

But I was between them and the border and en-
joying it less every second. I sneaked a quick look
around. What could I do? I watched Harry's wife
snuff out her cigarette into a cup on the table. Only it
wasn't out, it was smoking and smelling. Suddenly I
got another idea, my second one this month.

"Fire!" I yelled, grabbing the cup and throwing it
at the window. "Fire!"

They stumbled into one another as I pushed, shoved, ran out of that crowded room, dumping chairs behind me as they tried to grab me.

"Fire, help!" I yelled as I ran out the door. A small crowd began to gather now, milling around the trailer, as I charged full speed back to Ruff's stall. Uncle Wheeler was talking to Idamae.

"Didn't I tell you to listen for the national anthem?" Idamae put her hands on her hips and glared at me. "Don't tell me you don't recognize it? Terrific. He's got a tin ear, too."

"Uncle Wheeler," I gasped. "Ruff's owners aren't his owners at all. They stole him too. Get the sheriff, go to trailer 321. Lots of people—lots of smoke—" I was out of breath.

"Well, that sounds pretty peculiar." Uncle Wheeler scratched his chin.

"Don't let them get away," I yelled. "Please."

"Do as he says," Idamae bossed Uncle Wheeler. Then she grabbed me by the arm. "Come on, I saddled Ruff. We're next."

Somehow I got myself together on Ruff's back and then the rodeo announcer was calling our names. "Good luck," Idamae whispered, as we watched our steer run into the arena.

Now we charged in after him, our ropes whistling

above our heads. "Come on, Ruff, we're a team one last time," I yelled, feeling him gather strength as he ran. Then my rope went plop, right over the steer's horns and Idamae's rope was there at the other end, under his hind feet, neat as you please. Then we turned our horses to face the steer in a straight line, as it says to do in the rule book, with our ropes neat and taut.

"Time," we both screamed together and the audience came up on its feet, stamping and cheering. Idamae actually smiled at me as we rode out of the arena together.

The sheriff and Uncle Wheeler were waiting for us back at the stall. They had caught the man and woman who had stolen Ruff from his real owners down at Painted Horse Farms. In fact, the sheriff had just heard from Ruff's real owners and they were on their way to collect him and give me a reward. I couldn't have Ruff, of course, but they wondered if I'd be interested in one of Ruff's sons?

"You're going to own a real thoroughbred Paint," Idamae breathed. "Wow."

"Yeah." I could barely talk, but I just had to say, "Not bad for a dude with lots of spunk."

That did it. She couldn't stop laughing all the way home.

About the Author

Elizabeth Van Steenwyk, author of more than thirty-five books for young people, was born and educated in Galesburg, Illinois. A graduate of Knox College, she was inspired to write *Ghost in the Gym and Terror on the Rebound* from incidents that happened during her schoolhood days. She has lived with her husband and four children in San Marino, California for many years and teaches seminars on writing for young people at California Polytechnic State University.

About the Artist

Keith Neely attended the School of the Art Institute of Chicago and received a Bachelor of Fine Arts degree with honors from the Art Center College of Design, where he majored in illustration. He has worked as an art director, designer, and illustrator and has taught advertising illustration and advertising design at Biola College in La Mirada, California. Mr. Neely is currently a freelance illustrator whose work has appeared in numerous magazines, books, and advertisements. He lives with his wife and five children in Flossmoor, Illinois, a suburb of Chicago.